My Grandpa's Amazing INVENTIONS

RICHARD JOHNSON

templar publishing

This is me with my grandpa.
My grandpa is very old and very clever. At the bottom of the
garden, in his dark dusty workshop, he makes
the most marvellous things.

My grandpa is an INVENTOR!

One day a letter arrived for Grandpa.
This is what it said:

Dear Sir,

You have been invited to take part in...

The World's Latest and Greatest

Invention Contest

(Grandpa category)

Use your imagination and build
something amazing to win the

FIRST PRIZE TROPHY!

Grandpa scratched his head.

"What shall I build?" he wondered. Then Grandma had an idea.
"How about an **AMAZING-SPEAKA-ZOO-O-PHONE** gizmo that lets us
talk with the animals? Imagine chatting with a giraffe!
What would you ask it?"

"Hmm. That's been done before," said Grandpa. "What else?"

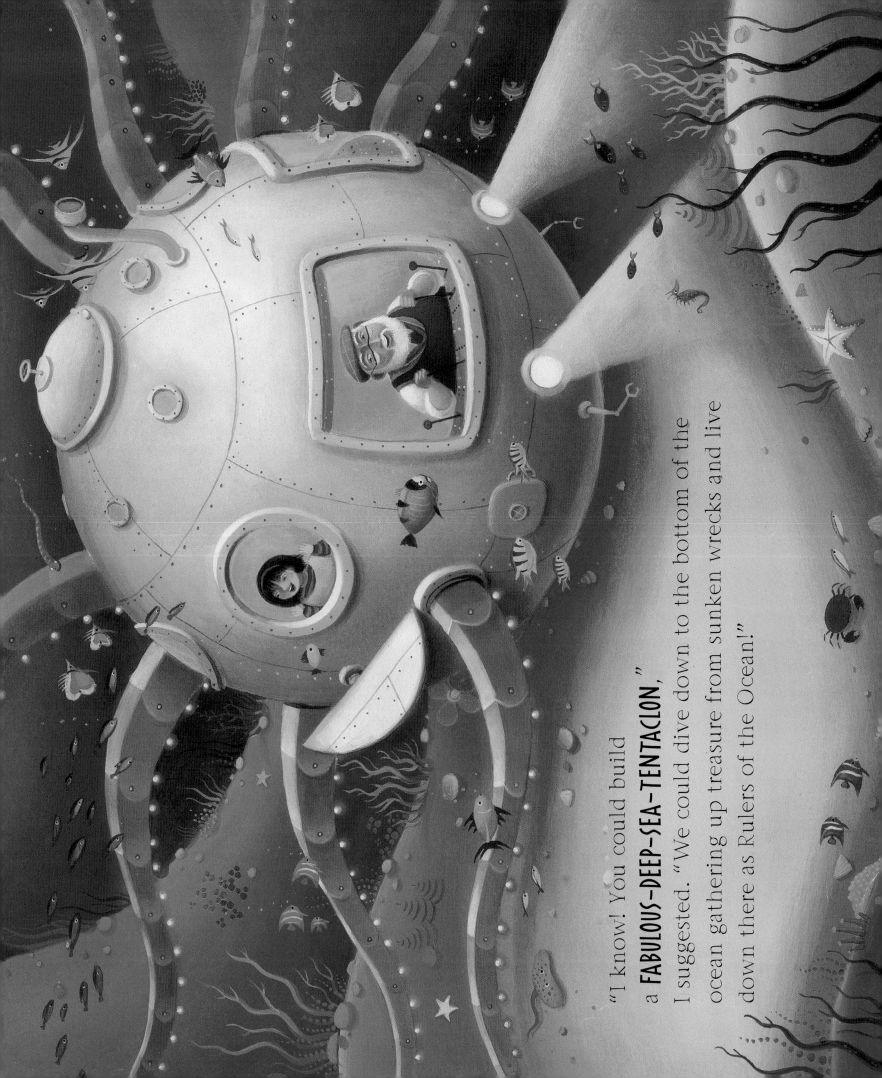

"I know! You could build
a **FABULOUS–DEEP–SEA–TENTACLON**,"
I suggested. "We could dive down to the bottom of the
ocean gathering up treasure from sunken wrecks and live
down there as Rulers of the Ocean!"

"Imagine a fine red **DOUBLE-DECKA-SPACE-BUS!**" Grandpa said dreamily.
"We could catch it at the end of our road and take a day trip
across the galaxy!
Picnic on the moon,
anyone?"

"I've heard the views
aren't bad!"

"Yeah! Or you could make us
SUPA-BOUNCY-HEATED-BALLOON-O-SUITS!" I said.
"We could bounce around the park
and never hurt ourselves
or get cold!"

"Or perhaps you could build me a **MULTI-ACTION-DIRTOID-DIGGA** to help with the gardening?" Grandma suggested.

"I could use it to burrow deep underground and spy on the neighbours' turnips!"

"What about making a
MAGNIFICENT–MAGNIFYING–BEAM–MACHINE
that can make things ten times bigger?" I said.

"You'd have to be careful where you pointed it, though!"
murmured Grandpa.

"Hey! I could build us some **FABULOUSLY-FEATHERED-MECHANICAL-FLIP-FLAPPERS!**" Grandpa said, waving his arms and leaping about. "We could fly with the birds, over the tallest towers and into the clouds! UP, UP and AWAY!"

It was getting late
when suddenly Grandpa shouted:
"I know exactly what I'll build!"
He rushed off down the garden path to his
workshop where he stayed all night,
hammering,
sawing,
banging and
crashing.

The next morning, a tired Grandpa
emerged from his workshop with a grin.
His mysterious machine was
hidden under a large
blanket.

We begged him to tell us
what he had made,
but he wouldn't.
"It's a secret," he winked.
"You'll have to wait
and see."

It was the day of the competition. While Grandpa made a few last-minute adjustments to his machine I decided to explore.

I saw a gizmo called the **FANCY-PANT-WASHING-WONDER-BOT**; a gadget called the **SUPER-DUPER-SELF-SOAPING-COPTER-BATH** and all sorts of other amazing things.

The World's Latest and Greatest *Invention Contest*

Then it was Grandpa's turn.

Everyone fell silent as they waited
for him to reveal his amazing invention...

"Ladies and gentlemen," announced Grandpa.
"I would like to present my incredible
STORY-TELLING-SHOWING-N-SMELLING-MARVELLOUS-MAGIC-MACHINE!"
He whisked away the blanket and flicked a switch.
The machine whirred into action.

The crowd were enthralled as Grandpa's invention
told them wonderful tales, accompanied by little pictures
and sound effects and even smells that drifted
amongst them.

Everyone clapped and cheered
and agreed that Grandpa's invention
should win the First Prize Trophy!

Later that evening, it was finally
my turn to try the story machine.
But when Grandpa switched it on,
all that came out was a puff of smoke...

"Crackle... POP!
Once upon a pigeon,
three bananas
cooked a game
of fish-fingers.
THE E-N-D."

The amazing
invention was broken.
"Oh dear," said Grandpa,
chuckling. "Never mind,
I think I had better tell you
a bedtime story of my own."

So Grandpa invented a wonderful story about a little girl
who owned a pair of Fabulously-Feathered-Mechanical-Flip-
Flappers, and flew round the world with them, having
all sorts of magical adventures.

"Who needs a story-telling machine?" I thought drowsily,
my eyes beginning to close, "I've got a..."

WUNDA-MARVELLOUS-CREATA-TASTIC-CRINKLE-WRINKLE-MAGIC-MAKING-GRANDPAPA!

The best Grandpa in all the world...

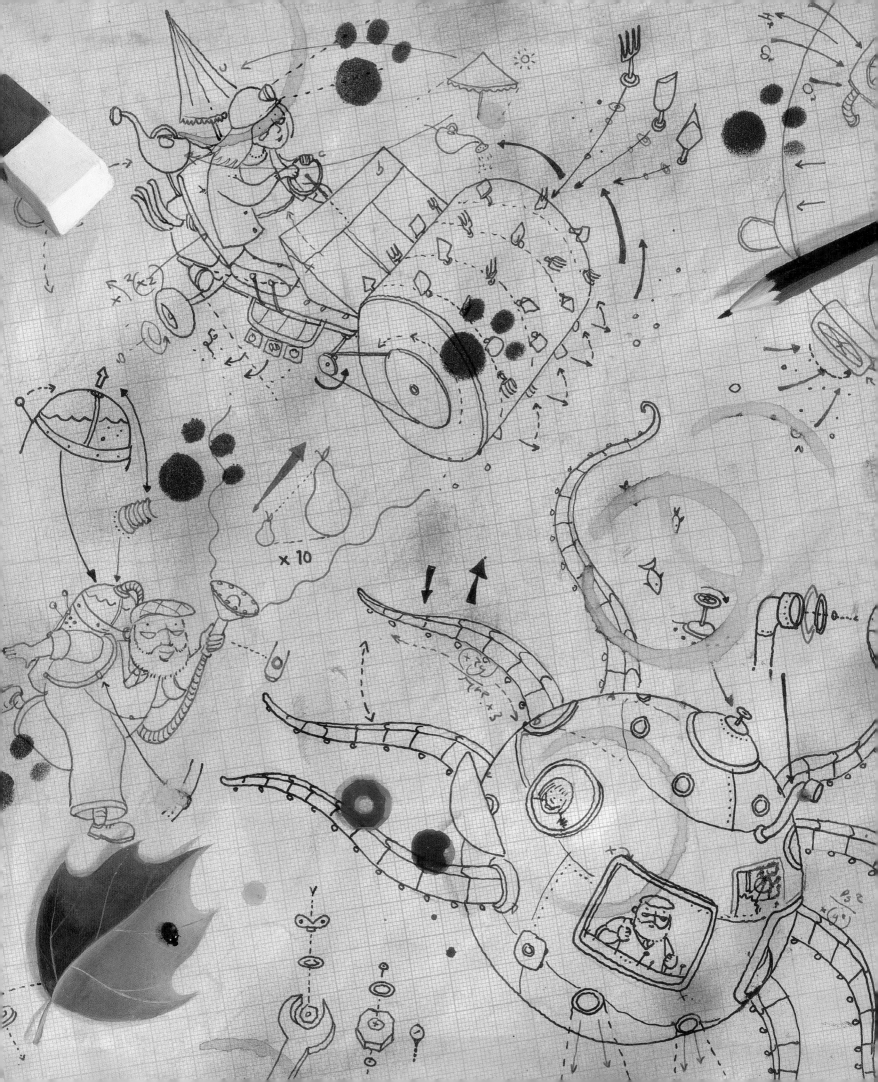